Look to the South

Look to the South

Renato Tranquilino

8Letters Bookstore and Publishing

CONTENTS

Many thanks, Mindanao, for your support of Pinoy Sci-Fi

Look to the South by Renato Clarete Tranquilino
Copyright © 2023
Printed in the Philippines
Look To The South is a work of science fiction. Names of people, places, events, businesses, and incidents are either products of the author's imagination or used in a fictitious manner. Any resemblance to persons, living or dead, or actual events is purely coincidental.

ISBN: 978-621-479-861-2

Cover and inside-cover artwork by Renato Tranquilino © 2023
Cover design and formatted by Elena Buncaras

I did a little compilation to thank the folks of Mindanao for supporting Pinoy Sci-Fi and my book "Fate of A Distant Future."

I hope it inspires the young ones to think that their ideas and dreams are a part of incredible advancements that await all of us in the future.

Rebirth from the Rubble

In the bustling city of Manila, a senator named Nate Domagoso found himself embroiled in the challenges of governance and the pursuit of a better future for his people. Amidst the constant demands and complex negotiations, a remarkable opportunity presented itself, one that could reshape the destiny of both Manila and the island of Mindanao.

Senator Nate Domagoso, a charismatic and determined leader, had long been concerned about Manila's overcrowding and strained resources. He envisioned a city that could thrive without the burden of overpopulation, pollution, and traffic congestion. The solution to his vision lay in the deep-rooted aspirations of the people of Mindanao, particularly the council of twelve, headed by Chairman Datu Hameradan.

Chairman Hameradan and his council had long sought autonomy for the region, envisioning a separate state with the power to govern its affairs, control its borders, and defend its coastal waters. Their dreams aligned with Senator Nate Domagoso's vision for Manila, and together they embarked on a journey to reshape the map of the Philippines.

Months of meticulous negotiations followed, fueled by a shared sense of purpose and a commitment to the well-being of their respective regions. Senator Nate Domagoso and Chairman Datu Hameradan tirelessly discussed the terms of an unprecedented arrangement. Finally, after long hours of deliberation, they reached a historic agreement that would change the fate of both Manila and Mindanao forever.

With a shared sense of purpose, Senator Nate Domagoso and Chairman Dato Hameradan embarked on a journey of collaboration and negotiation. After months of intense discussions, they reached an extraordinary arrangement that would forever alter the landscape of the Philippines.

The agreement entailed the relocation of Manila to the vibrant city of Davao, situated on the shores of Mindanao. This monumental move would provide a fresh start for Manila and grant full autonomy to the region, complete with its border controls, army, and navy to safeguard its coastal waters.

The announcement of this bold plan sent shockwaves across the nation. Skepticism and doubt mingled with hope and anticipation. Some questioned the feasibility of such a colossal undertaking. In contrast, others saw it as a chance for Manila to rise from the ashes and for Mindanao to chart its destiny.

As the relocation commenced, the nation witnessed

extraordinary unity and resilience. The people of Manila, battered but unbroken, embraced the idea of a fresh start in Davao. They packed their belongings, bid farewell to their devastated city, and journeyed south with trepidation and hope.

Meanwhile, in Mindanao, preparations for the arrival of their newfound brethren were underway. The infrastructure of Davao was expanded, providing ample space and resources for the rebirth of Manila. The city's residents welcomed their new compatriots with open arms, knowing they were building a future forged from shared experiences and determination.

Years passed, and the transformation became evident. Manila, reborn in Davao, blossomed with resilience and vibrancy. Gleaming structures and a sense of renewal gradually replaced the scars of the earthquake. Mindanao, now an autonomous region, thrived, nurturing its identity while safeguarding its coastal waters with a strong and self-sufficient defense.

The relocation of Manila and granting autonomy to Mindanao proved to be a turning point in Philippine history. It showcased the power of collaboration, resilience, and visionary leadership. Senator Nate Domagoso and Chairman Dato Hameradan became revered figures, their names forever etched in the hearts of the people they served.

The story of Manila's rebirth and Mindanao's autonomy symbolized hope and triumph, reminding future generations that even in the face of unthinkable devastation, unity, and the unwavering human spirit can forge a path toward a brighter tomorrow and a message to the world:

Look to the South...

2

A Flame Never Extinguished

In the heart of Maynilad, the new capital of the Philippines in Mindanao, located in Davao City, a group of die-hard old Manilenos clung to an unwavering hope that burned bright despite the seemingly insurmountable odds. Their beloved capital had been leased to a foreign country for a century, leaving Luzon in the grip of an unfamiliar power. But these resilient individuals refused to let their dreams fade away.

As the years passed, the flame of their hope flickered on, nurtured by a steadfast belief that one day, Manila would return to its rightful place in Luzon. They drew strength from each other's stories and memories, cherishing the city's glorious past while envisioning a future in which it would be restored to its former grandeur. But most importantly, the hope that one day, Senator Nate Domagoso will wake up from his coma-induced recovery and right what was wrong.

They still remember the tragedy that had struck Senator Nate Domagoso, a figure revered by the old Manilenos and once hope for the entire country. The news shook the community to its core, threatening to extinguish their hope for a speedy recovery of the country from the great quake of 2508.

But fate, it seemed, had other plans. Mindanao's finest doctors, aware of the significance Senator Nate held in the hearts of many Filipinos, took swift action. Working with the Mindanao State Intelligence Bureau (MSIB) began transporting the injured couple to the Davao First District Hospital. A remarkable combination of human and AI-robot doctors labored tirelessly to mend their broken bodies.

With a delicate touch, the doctors induced Senator Nate and his girlfriend into a deep coma, a necessary step in their journey toward recovery. As the believers anxiously waited, they held onto the belief that Senator Nate's awakening could nullify the Article-12 vote cast on his behalf—the vote that had sealed Manila's lease to the foreign country.

As Senator Nate Domagoso and his girlfriend remained in their induced comas, days turned into weeks and weeks into months. Yet, even in the face of uncertainty, the old Manilenos refused to let their hope waver. They stood united, a tight-knit community, sharing stories of their city's past splendor and nurturing their dreams for its eventual return.

Nate Domagoso - politician

Nardong Itim- gentleman assassin of Nate Domagoso

Within the walls of Davao First District Hospital, the combined efforts of human and AI-robot doctors brought healing to the broken bodies of Senator Nate and his girlfriend. Their expertise, guided by the integration of advanced technology and compassionate care, worked tirelessly to repair the extensive damage inflicted by the accident.

The believers continued to pray, their hopes intertwined with the rhythmic beeping of the hospital machines. They clung to the possibility that one day, Senator Nate would awaken from his induced slumber, ready to confront the challenges ahead. Their unwavering belief in his strength and resilience propelled them forward, even when doubt threatened to take hold.

And so, the story of the die-hard old Manilenos persisted, an indomitable flame that refused to be extinguished. Their unwavering faith, supported by the expertise of Mindanao's finest doctors, sustained the flickering beacon of hope for Manila's return to Luzon. As they awaited the awakening of their beloved senator, they held steadfast to the belief that miracles could happen, breathing life into the age-old truth that where there is hope, there is always a way forward.

As the city of Maynilad buzzed with anticipation and the old Manilenos clung to their flickering hope, another remarkable story unfolded in the shadows, away from prying eyes. Senator Elizabeth Robredo, presumed dead by the world, found refuge in a clandestine hideout provided by the Mindanao Special Intelligence Bureau (MSIB). Nestled on one of the remote islands off the southern coast of Mindanao, she observed the unfolding events from her secret situation room alongside her dedicated staff.

The news of Senator Robredo's disappearance had sent shockwaves through the nation. Many believed her to be a casualty of the political turmoil that had engulfed the country because of Article 12. Little did they know that she had taken refuge with the MSIB, a select group of operatives committed to protecting and ensuring her safety.

In the hidden enclave, Senator Robredo's situation room served as the nerve center of their operations. High-tech screens lined the walls, displaying many live feeds, intelligence reports, and maps. Her staff, composed of loyal and trusted individuals, worked tirelessly to gather information, assess risks, and strategize the next steps.

As Senator Robredo watched the unfolding events from her secure hideout, a mix of emotions flooded her heart. She felt a profound responsibility towards her people and her loved country. She yearned to join the coalition for Manila's return to Luzon, to stand alongside her friend Nate and the old Manilenos and fight for their shared dream. However, she knew that her presence in the public eye could compromise the mission and jeopardize their cause.

Senator Robredo coordinated with her staff from her hidden sanctuary, exchanging information and insights. They analyzed the political landscape, evaluated the strength of the old Manilenos movement, and considered the best course of action. Every decision in that situation room was calculated, rooted in their unwavering commitment to the vision of Manila's return to Luzon and restoring their nation's pride.

Days turned into weeks, and Senator Robredo's resolve only grew stronger. From her secret hideout, she prepared for the day when the time would come to reveal herself to the world. She knew that her return could ignite a powerful wave of support, strengthening the cause and revitalizing the hope of the old Manilenos.

In the depths of her situation room, Senator Robredo studied maps of Manila, its streets etched into her memory. She strategized, planned, and envisioned a future where the capital would be restored, and the city's heartbeat would again resonate in Luzon.

And so, hidden away on the remote island, Senator Elizabeth Robredo, presumed dead by the world, continued to watch, plan, and prepare. The unfolding events fueled her determination and strengthened her resolve. From her situation room, she stood ready to emerge, to join the fight and lend her voice to the chorus of those who longed for Manila's return. The time would come when she would step out of the shadows, for she knew that her presence would be a catalyst with her friend Nate, breathing new life into the flickering flame of hope that burned within the hearts of the old Manilenos.

3

The Good Dr. Katherine De Guzman

D r. Katherine De Guzman, an accomplished exo-biologist from General Santos Space City in the Philippines, possessed an insatiable curiosity that propelled her into space exploration. Armed with her extensive education from the prestigious Cambridge School of Xeno-biology, she joined the groundbreaking Kalawakan I mission, setting her sights on unraveling the mysteries of distant planets.

On their premature attempted entry into Pacain's atmosphere due to a software malfunction, the crew of Kalawakan I tried in vain to penetrate with sensors the thick clouds of the planet Pacain. Dr. De Guzman's excitement grew as she prepared to delve into the unexplored depths of this alien world. Armed with state-of-the-art equipment and a thirst for discovery, she prepared her gear and staff for a mission that would test the limits of her scientific prowess.

As the ship entered Pacain's atmosphere, the crew dangled

a camera from the starship and lowered it through the thick clouds to capture the planet's terrain so the staff could decide on a safe place to land. Dr. De Guzman meticulously analyzed the data streams from the cameras, sifting through images of Pacain's majestic landscapes and exotic flora. But one set of photographs, taken just before a mysterious incident, revealed something truly extraordinary.

In the last few photos snapped by the camera, before it was unexpectedly lost, Dr. De Guzman noticed peculiar shapes emerging from the cloud cover. An inexplicable mix of excitement and trepidation washed over her as she zoomed in, her eyes widening in disbelief. There, amidst the clouds, were the unmistakable teeth that resembled that of a carnivorous dinosaur—flying T-Rexs.

The realization hit her like a thunderclap. The existence of these astonishing creatures, soaring through the skies of Pacain, held profound implications for our understanding of extraterrestrial life. But as one of these majestic creatures devoured the ship's camera, Dr. De Guzman yearned to witness them firsthand from the ground.

Days later, after the starship landed on Pacain's surface, Dr. De Guzman's anticipation reached a fever pitch. Stepping onto the alien terrain, she gazed at the cloud-filled sky, hoping to glimpse the elusive flying T-Rexs. A mix of wonder and anticipation filled her heart as she awaited the spectacle she had only seen through those final photographs.

Suddenly, a deep sound of shrieks filled the air, and her eyes fixed on the sky. In a breathtaking display, the flying T-Rexs (though they looked more like butikis or small salamanders found in ancient Philippine homes with T-rex teeth) materialized from the clouds, their mighty wings spanning wide, casting shadows upon the land below. Dr. De Guzman's heart soared with awe and amazement as she watched these magnificent creatures navigate the sky with grace and power.

At that moment, Dr. De Guzman realized that sometimes the universe's wonders reveal themselves unexpectedly. The photographs, captured by the camera that met its untimely demise, had ignited a flame of curiosity within her that could only be quenched by experiencing the creatures firsthand.

Witnessing the flying T-Rexs in all their splendor from the ground of Pacain, Dr. Katherine De Guzman's spirit was invigorated, fueling her determination to explore the mysteries of the cosmos. With each discovery, she would continue to push the boundaries of scientific knowledge, unlocking the universe's secrets, one breathtaking encounter at a time.

As the esteemed doctor observed the mesmerizing images of the swirling clouds on the planet Pacain, a peculiar thought crossed her mind. The captivating phenomenon reminded her of the biblical Manna, the divine sustenance that had descended upon the deserts of Egypt, nourishing the exiled people of Moses. It was a theory she once contemplated and discussed with her colleagues, only to be ridiculed and dismissed. The experience had left her hesitant ever to broach the topic again. Still, in this solitary moment of reflection, she couldn't help but revisit the notion, allowing her mind to wander through the unexplored realms of possibility.

4 |

Mindanao State: A Nexus of Innovation and Controversy

As centuries passed and the capital city Manila was eventually repatriated to Luzon, the island of Mindanao flourished, emerging as a leading center for Food and Drug Research. Mindanao State, renowned for its intellectual prowess, became a powerhouse in scientific advancements, rivaling even the research facilities of the Mars One city on the red planet.

The pharmaceutical laboratories of Mindanao State spearheaded the development of life-saving vaccines and cutting-edge techniques for enhancing food production. Their breakthroughs helped address global challenges in health and agriculture, positioning Mindanao as a hub of innovation and progress.

However, alongside these remarkable achievements, Mindanao State also gained notoriety for its advancements in Nanite technology. These tiny, self-replicating machines revolutionized various fields, from medicine to manufacturing. Mindanao State's expertise in Nanite technology surpassed regional boundaries, drawing both admiration and concern from the global community.

Yet, it wasn't only scientific marvels that emanated from Mindanao State. Unfortunately, the island became Southeast Asia's primary source for advanced weapon technology developments. Their prowess in this field often stirred international controversy and caught the world's ire. Mindanao State's love-hate relationship with the global community and the planetary union became an enduring characteristic of their complex identity.

Amidst this backdrop of admiration, controversy, and contradiction, the Multo weapons division of Mercel Corporation made a significant decision. Recognizing Mindanao State's expertise in various forms of advanced technology, Multo established its weapons division headquarters on the island. This move would benefit Multo and further consolidate Mindanao's reputation as a technological powerhouse.

With Multo's weapons division taking root in Mindanao, the island's scientific landscape underwent a dynamic transformation. The fusion of Multo's resources and expertise with Mindanao State's intellectual prowess led to unprecedented advancements in weaponry. Cutting-edge research facilities sprouted across the island, fostering innovation and collaboration.

The arrival of Multo sparked debates and controversy among the people of Mindanao. While some celebrated the economic opportunities and technological advancements that came with Multo's presence, others voiced concerns about the ethical implications of developing advanced weaponry. The love-hate relationship with the world intensified as Mindanao State reached the crossroads of progress and responsibility.

Meanwhile, Multo's weapons division, driven by Mindanao's wealth of talent and resources, pushed the boundaries of weapon technology. Their innovations in weaponry ranged from precision-guided systems to next-generation defensive technologies, solidifying Mindanao's reputation as a formidable force in the field.

As the years went by, the world closely watched the developments emerging from Mindanao State. The island's dual role as a center for groundbreaking scientific research and advanced weapon technology continued to draw both admiration and skepticism.

Mindanao State's expertise in diverse forms of advanced technology became a defining characteristic of the island's identity. Pursuing scientific progress remained at the core of Mindanao State's mission, even as they grappled with their advancements' ethical implications and global repercussions.

Despite the controversies surrounding their involvement in weapons development, Mindanao State maintained its commitment to driving positive change. They actively sought collaborations and partnerships, engaging in joint projects to utilize their technological advancements for peaceful purposes. Their scientists and researchers consistently explored ways to leverage their expertise in Nanite technology, pharmaceutical breakthroughs, and agricultural enhancements to address global challenges.

Mindanao State's journey of innovation, controversy, and reconciliation epitomized the complex nature of progress in the modern world. Their love-hate relationship with the global community served as a reminder of the delicate balance between harnessing advanced technology for the betterment of humanity and ensuring its responsible use.

As Mindanao State's reputation continued to evolve, the island stood poised to navigate the intricate terrain of global politics and scientific advancements. Their unwavering commitment to knowledge and innovation propelled them forward, shaping a future where Mindanao's contributions would be recognized for their scientific prowess and dedication to creating a better world.

As the early days of colonization on the distant planet Pacain unfolded, an urgent call for supplies and weaponry echoed across the void of space. Kalawakan I, the first colony established on Pacain, reached out for assistance, and Mindanao State answered the call with unwavering determination.

While the rest of the world viewed the colonization efforts skeptically, believing they had been deceived by Mercel and the United Regions of the Philippines, Mindanao State saw the situation differently. They recognized the vast potential and untapped opportunities that lay beyond the confines of Earth. Mindanao State stood firmly in support of the colonists, embracing the vision of a new frontier that could bring unimaginable benefits to the entire nation.

Drawing upon their influential position, Mindanao State embarked on a passionate lobbying campaign, rallying the different autonomous regions to stand united in their support. Their message resonated with leaders across the country, who began to envision a future where the Philippines would conquer a planet, forging a legacy that surpassed their wildest dreams.

The stage was set for a remarkable event—a declaration of steadfast support on the Philippine Independence Day, a little over six months after the clandestine launch of the secret first colony on Pacain. Mindanao State Intelligence Agency (MSIA), an organization renowned for its strategic acumen, guaranteed the success of this audacious endeavor. With the persistent backing of Mindanao State, Mercel and the United Regions of the Philippines stood up to the scrutiny and opposition of the planetary union.

The momentous decision to aid the colonists on Pacain marked a turning point in the United Regions of the Philippines' history. It demonstrated the nation's unwavering determination, courageously pushing beyond the confines of Earth to establish a foothold on another world. Mindanao State's resolute support became a cornerstone of this endeavor, bolstering the collective spirit and resolve of the Philippine people.

The world watched as the URP, led by the indomitable spirit of Mindanao State, embarked on an extraordinary journey of conquest and exploration. The decision to stand firm in the face of skepticism and opposition ignited a beacon of hope and unity throughout the nation.

As supplies and weaponry were mobilized, a new chapter in the human saga unfolded. The colonists of Kalawakan I, buoyed by the support of their compatriots, embarked on their mission with renewed vigor, ready to face the challenges of Pacain head-on.

In this pivotal moment, Mindanao State's unwavering support set the stage for a remarkable future, where the spirit of the Philippines transcended planetary boundaries and embraced the infinite possibilities that awaited them among the stars.

And thus, in kindergarten schools all across the nation, an ancient poem from a long forgotten and obscure book that embodied the hope of very distant ancestors to reach the stars, the children would always start their day with the poem done as a song:

> *We were all once from stardust,*
> *and to that, we will return.*
> *For Pinoys to reach distant stars,*

is not just inevitable,
but just a case of going home.

So here we come with great hope,
A cobbled band of few.
We're coming home,
all battered and weary,
with six hundred million in tow.

-end-

Renato Clarete Tranquilino is a Filipino-Australian IT Professional interested in sci-fi fantasy films and writing stories. Playing League of Legends is his other pastime. He dreams of traveling the world and visiting places of interest related to science fiction and urban fantasy novels.